THE MYSTERY

AT

Motown

Editor: Janice Baker
Assistant Editor: Beverly Melasi
Cover Design: John Hanson
Content Design: Randolyn Friedlander
Photo Credits: Wikipedia.com

Gallopade International is introducing SAT words that kids need to know in each
new book that we publish. The SAT words are bold in the story. Look for each
word in the special SAT glossary. Happy Learning!!

Gallopade is proud to be a member and supporter of these educational organizations
and associations:

American Booksellers Association
American Library Association
International Reading Association
National Association for Gifted Children
The National School Supply and Equipment Association
The National Council for the Social Studies
Museum Store Association
Association of Partners for Public Lands
Association of Booksellers for Children
Association for the Study of African American Life and History
National Alliance of Black School Educators

Once upon a time...

You two really are characters, that's all I've got to say!

Yes you are! And, of course I choose you! But what should I write about?

National parks!

 SCARY PLACES!

FAMOUS PLACES!

FUN PLACES!

Disney World!

New York City!

Dracula's Castle

GRAND CANYON

On the *Mystery Girl* airplane ...

I can FLY US anyWHERE!

Mystery Girl

Or aboard the *Mimi!*

Mimi

Take me to the Forbidden City!

Or by surfboard, rickshaw, motorbike, camel ...

All great ideas! I can put a lot of history,

MYSTERY,

legend, lore, and laughs in the books! We can use other boys and girls in the books. It will be educational and fun!

Good stuff!

And can you put some cool stuff online? Like a Book Club and a Scavenger Hunt and a Map so we can track our adventures?

Of course!

And can cousins Avery and Ella and Evan and some of our friends be in the books?

Of course!

Can I apply?

LET'S GO!

$\mathcal{A}$nd so, Mimi, Papa, Christina, and Grant took off aboard the *Mystery Girl* and America's National Mystery Book Series—where the adventure is real and so are the characters! —was born.

START YOUR ADVENTURE TODAY!

1
WHAT IS A MOTOWN?

"Look! There's the Ambassador Bridge!" Papa shouted as he began the *Mystery Girl's* descent into Detroit, Michigan. The little red and white airplane tipped to the right as he made a wide turn. He spoke for a minute to the air traffic controller at the Willow Run Airport where they would land.

Mimi was excited, too, and turned in her seat. "The Ambassador Bridge is the gateway to Motown," Mimi told Christina and Grant. She and Papa had been to Detroit many times, but it was still a thrill to look down on the magnificent bridge that connected the United States to Canada.

Christina and Grant often traveled with their mystery-writing grandmother. Mimi's latest book was to be set in Motown, and she was already pumped up with the excitement of beginning a new mystery. Their grandfather, Papa, flew the family wherever Mimi's mysteries took them.

Grant, who had been dozing for a while, opened his eyes and stretched. "Is the 'Mo' in Motown like 'mow,' as in, 'mow the lawn'?" he wanted to know. "Do they have a lot of grass there?"

"No, Grant," Mimi replied. She held up her hand and pointed to a spot on it. "Motown is right here."

"What, do you want a high-five, Mimi?" Christina raised her own hand to give her one.

"No," Mimi said, smiling. "I'm just showing you where Detroit is. The state of Michigan is shaped like a mitten. Residents can show people where they live by pointing to a spot on their left hand. Detroit is in the lower portion of the thumb, and is the automotive capital of the world! Motown is a nickname for the 'Motor City.'"

"Why is Detroit called the Motor City?" Grant asked.

"Well," Mimi explained, "it's because of Detroit's association with Henry Ford. His assembly line idea for automobile production changed how cars were made. Other car companies followed his idea and were also located in Detroit."

"And," Mimi added, "Motown is the home of Motown Records where the 'Motown Sound' was born."

Christina was excited. She loved music. "Is that a rock group, Mimi?" she asked.

Mimi laughed. "No, honey," she replied. "The Motown Sound was one of Detroit's great contributions to the music world."

The plane was descending, so Mimi checked her seatbelt and smoothed the skirt of her red suit so it wouldn't wrinkle. She reminded Christina and Grant to check their seatbelts too.

"Now, where was I? Oh yes, this afternoon we're going visit the legendary Motown Museum, Hitsville U.S.A.," Mimi said. "A very good friend of mine is the curator there, and she invited us to come!"

As soon as the kids heard the word 'museum,' they groaned. They liked museums, but it was too beautiful a day to spend indoors.

"It'll be fun, I promise," Mimi said. "To set foot in the place where so many music greats recorded their hits just gives me goose bumps." Mimi slid the sleeve of her red suit jacket back so the kids could see the tiny bumps on her skin.

"FSSSSST!" Radio static cut in. "Little red and white bird, you are cleared for landing, over."

"Roger that," Papa said into his radio. He turned to wink at the kids. "We'll have a lot to see and do while we're in Detroit," Papa told them. "From here we're going to Lafayette Coney Island for Coney dogs."

"Awesome!" Grant exclaimed. "Huh? What the heck is a Coney dog?"

"Ahhh...one of my fondest memories of Detroit," Papa said. "Coney dogs are to Detroit what apple pie is to America." He closed his eyes for a second as if to savor the memory. "Anyway, they're plump, juicy hot dogs smothered in chili and onions. Oh, and they're served with another personal favorite— chili cheese fries!"

"Oh, yes," remarked Mimi, "to go along with Papa's cast iron stomach!"

Papa winked at Mimi. "Point taken," he said with a chuckle. He reached over and flicked a few switches on the dashboard.

"Now, I'm reeeeallly hungry," Grant complained. He pulled on his hair and stretched his arms wide, making his blonde hair stick up in tufts.

"Oh, now there's a surprise," Christina commented.

Papa inhaled deeply, as if he could already smell the chili and onions. "We'll be going to lunch shortly. But first, let's set the old girl down and put her to bed."

"He means the plane," Mimi said, at the quizzical look the kids gave Papa.

Christina gazed out the window at the green landscape coming closer and closer. *Motown, here we come!* she thought.

2
YANKEES AND AIRPLANES

Papa held Mimi's hand as she climbed down the steps of the *Mystery Girl*. "My friend Joe will be here any minute to meet us," Papa explained. "He's a member of the Yankee Air Museum here, where they build and restore old war planes. You'll like him a lot. He's an 86-year-old retired World War II flight officer, and he always has an entertaining story to tell."

"I love making model airplanes!" said Grant.

A green golf cart whizzed up to meet the family. Its driver wore tinted glasses and a blue Yankee Air Museum jacket and hat. He hopped out of the front seat to greet them, shaking hands with Mimi and Papa.

Grant walked right up to Joe. "I know who you are," Grant said. "Joe, right?"

"How'd you know?" Joe asked, as if surprised.

"It says so on your belt buckle," Grant replied, pointing.

"So it does," Joe laughed, patting Grant on his head. He looked at Papa. "How about a quick tour of the Yankee Air Museum, and then meet my crew?" At Papa's nod, Joe led the family across the tarmac to a massive airplane hangar.

Joe pointed towards the airport runway. "Willow Run Airport was built by the Ford Motor Company during World War II to serve as an airfield for their B-24 bomber plant," he explained. "They used Henry Ford's automotive assembly line technique, and were able to produce one B-24 every 59 minutes."

"That's a lot of planes!" Grant shouted.

Inside the building were several restored planes, and some airplane cockpit training simulators.

Grant raced to one of the simulators and peeked inside. His hands itched to touch all those dials, switches, and levers. Tossing his backpack to the floor, he hopped inside, grabbed the control wheel, and started making plane sounds. "EEEERRRRMMM!" His voice echoed loudly, and everyone slapped their hands over their ears.

Papa tapped on the outside of the cockpit door. "OK, Ace. Come out of there before our eardrums burst."

With a reluctant "Yes, sir," Grant shuffled back to join the group.

Joe motioned to the open area where his crew was working. "Please excuse our dust. We just moved into this new hangar," he said. "Our old one burned down in 2004."

"I remember reading about that fire," Papa said. "I was so happy to hear that the *Yankee Lady* bomber was saved through the heroic efforts of museum volunteers."

Joe motioned them over to his workbench. "Yes, we were very lucky indeed, but everything else inside the hanger was destroyed, including the Waco tube glider we were restoring," Joe said. "And some of us had donated our old uniforms and artifacts from World War II to the museum. Those can never be replaced."

Grant was mesmerized, lunch totally forgotten now. "Did it take a long time to build your glider, Mr. Joe?"

"Over twelve years, Grant," Joe said.

"Gosh, that's awful!" Grant exclaimed, his eyes downcast.

Joe saw Grant's serious expression and didn't want him to look so sad. "Don't worry. We picked ourselves up and started building again," he said.

Joe pointed to a World War I SPAD fighter plane in various stages of completion. "Here's our newest project," he said. Three men were busy fitting a wing to the side of the plane. "Meet my crew, Harry, Richard, and Wild Bill!" The men smiled and waved. "With us working out in the open like this, people can come here and watch her being built, piece by piece."

"Do many people come to the Yankee Air Museum?" Mimi asked.

"Yes, thousands, actually," Joe said. "We have air shows several times a year." He tapped his chest. "I'm the docent here, so I speak to hundreds of Boy and Girl Scouts and others just interested in old war planes. We get a lot of new members that way.

"Come to think of it," Joe continued, "I have a little something you might like." He searched around on his workbench, picked up a folded T-shirt, and handed it to Grant. "Now you're an official junior member of the Yankee Air Museum! I hope you'll come back when you grow up so you can help us restore some war birds too."

Grant held up the shirt with a picture of the *Yankee Lady* bomber on the front. "Wow! Thanks, Mr. Joe!" he said.

Joe wiped his hands on a red rag and tucked it in his back pocket. "So where are you guys heading from here?" he asked.

"We're going to lunch, then on to the Motown Museum—Hitsville U.S.A.," Mimi replied.

"Well, that's just great!" Joe said. "Oh, hey, be sure to tell old Gus that Joe says hello. He's the tour guide at the museum, and he's almost as old as I am," Joe said with a chuckle.

"You know someone from the Motown Museum?" Grant asked.

"Sure. Old Gus and I go way back," Joe said. "Actually, he's a member of the Yankee Air Museum too. He was just here last week." Joe rubbed his chin. "He used to be a singer, and a pretty good one at that. Wrote a song, too, as I recall, but someone stole it before he could record it. Anyway, he said some strange things have been going on at the museum lately."

Christina's ears perked up. "What kind of strange things, Mr. Joe?"

Joe tapped his cheek. "Well, it seems there have been some eerie noises coming from the basement of the museum late at night."

Christina was even more interested now. She was fond of mysteries and riddles, so this was right up her alley. "Like ghosts or a haunting?" she asked.

Joe shrugged his shoulders. "Well, I wouldn't know about all that. Just strange sounds like chairs scraping, crashing noises, and moaning." He lined up some screwdrivers on his workbench. "Mr. Tom, the night watchman, says he's checked it out several times, but doesn't see or hear anything while he's there." Joe smiled at the kids. "But, you just never know, do you?"

"Well," Papa clapped his hands together. "I think we've taken up enough of Mr. Joe's time. Let's get moving so we can chow down on those Coney dogs!" With that, the family headed out the door.

Grant looked around. "Oh, hey, I forgot my backpack!" he shouted. He ran over to the simulator and grabbed his backpack by its straps. On the floor was a scrap of paper. "Oops, must have fallen out," he said. Grant slipped it into the pocket on the front of his shirt.

As the taxi pulled away, the family waved good-bye to Mr. Joe. Grant pressed his nose to the window until he could no longer see him. He felt that he'd made a friend for life.

Grant turned to Christina. "Hey," he whispered. "Maybe it won't be so bad visiting a museum if there's a mystery to solve!"

3
CONEY CHAMPS

The bright yellow taxi stopped in front of the Lafayette Coney Island restaurant. Papa's mouth watered at the thought of devouring one (OK, maybe two) Coney dogs. He pushed his Stetson cowboy hat back on his head. "Let's not keep them doggies waitin'!" he joked.

Once they stepped inside, they were immediately bombarded by the sights, sounds, and **potent** aromas of the noisy restaurant. Energetic waitresses barked orders to the kitchen staff, and a Tigers baseball game blared on the big screen TV on the wall.

As he studied the menu, Grant made smacking sounds with his mouth every time he saw an item he liked. "I want those chili cheese fries with my Coney dog, 'cause I'm really, really hungry," he told the waitress.

"Gotcha covered, little man," she said, smiling.

Soon, plates heaped with Coney dogs drowning in chili and onions arrived in front of Papa and Grant.

"Ahhh, just smell that! It was definitely worth the wait," Papa said, leaning over his plate to savor the aroma. He sank his teeth into his Coney dog and sighed. "That's what I'm talking about!" he mumbled between bites.

While they ate, Christina and Grant discussed what Mr. Joe had told them regarding the Motown Museum and the eerie noises at night. "It seriously creeps me out," Christina admitted. She didn't like monsters or supernatural things.

"Not me," Grant said, waving a fry at her. "I can't wait to get there!" He shoveled more fries into his mouth. "It'll be soooo cool!"

"Well, I guess things that go bump in the night don't necessarily mean ghosts," Christina said hesitantly. Suddenly, she looked at Grant's shirt and asked, "Hey, what's that sticking out of your pocket?"

"Huh? Oh, this?" Grant slid the scrap of paper out of his pocket. "It was on the floor next to my backpack when I went back to get it." He examined it more closely. "Hey, this isn't mine. It looks like part of a photograph that was torn into pieces."

He handed it to his sister. "See?" he asked. "It looks like somebody's shoes." Grant turned the picture over. There was writing on the back:

> *He walked away from someone in need.*

Grant snapped his fingers and jumped to his feet. "Hey, maybe it's a clue!"

"A clue to what?" Christina asked.

Grant shrugged his shoulders. "I don't know yet, but I just have that feeling."

Christina tugged on his arm. "Yeah, well, sit down until that feeling goes away. We don't need everyone in the restaurant to know," she whispered, looking at Mimi and Papa who were watching the Tigers game. "Just put it away for now, OK?"

"OK," Grant said. He stuffed the piece of torn photo back into his front pocket. After that, the kids finished their lunch in silence.

Papa declared he and Grant to be "Coney Champs," and used a napkin to wipe his chin free of chili and mustard. He tipped his Stetson back on his head, pushed back his chair, and stretched his long legs. "I may never move again," he groaned, patting his belly.

Grant was full, too, and thought about letting out a big belch.

Mimi leaned over and warned, "Don't even think about it."

Grant looked stunned. "How does she do that?" he asked Papa.

Papa laughed and tousled Grant's blond curls. "You should know by now that nothing gets past your grandmother!"

Mimi and Christina were devouring a Sanders hot fudge cream puff. The gooey, chocolate fudge confection was a Detroit specialty. "And you know," Mimi said to Christina with a wink, "there are no calories if you share!"

Mimi licked fudge off her thumb. "As soon as we finish this delightful dessert, we'll head over to Hitsville U.S.A."

"And find out more about the mystery at Motown," Grant whispered to Christina. They gave each other a high-five.

No one saw the man peer into the restaurant window and look around intently until he found Grant and Christina. He nodded and slipped away.

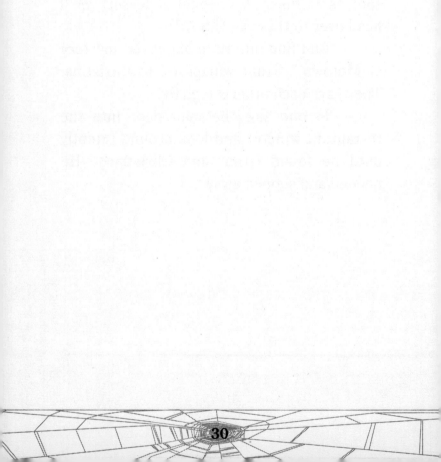

4

HITSVILLE U.S.A.!

The street in front of Hitsville U.S.A. was lined with tour buses. Mimi led the children up the sidewalk to a cheerful white house with blue trim.

"This is it?" Christina said. "Are you sure? It just looks like somebody's home!"

Mimi nodded. "This is the place where it all began! Follow me!"

Two friendly guards stood at the doors as the family entered. Because no picture-taking was allowed in the museum, they quickly scanned Grant's backpack and the girls' purses, then waved them through.

A tall woman in a bright tangerine dress rushed up to greet the family. Helene had been the curator of Hitsville U.S.A. for more than twenty years, and had known Mimi even longer. They both squealed like two schoolgirls and hugged each other tightly.

Papa shook hands with Helene, and introduced Christina and Grant.

"Oh, how wonderful to see you all," Helene said, dabbing at the tears in her eyes. "Mimi, I'm so glad you contacted me when you decided to write a mystery here. We're hosting a Motown Review on Friday and I'd love for all of you to come!"

"What's a Motown Review?" asked Grant.

Helene smiled and said, "The original Motown Reviews were held in the Fox Theater downtown to showcase popular Motown singers, like The Temptations, Smokey and the Miracles, and Diana Ross and The Supremes, just to name a few." Helene handed Mimi a colorful flyer. "Our Motown Review will be held in Hart Plaza. We'll have music, dancing, and films of the legendary Motown entertainers in concert shown on large TV screens throughout the evening."

"Count us in!" Mimi exclaimed.

Helene clapped her hands. "Great!" She turned to Christina and Grant. "I can't wait for you to meet my two grandchildren. They're hanging around here somewhere." She paused as a boy and a girl entered the room. "Look! Here they are now!"

She took the young boy's hand. "Will and Denielle, I'd like you to meet some friends of mine, Mimi, Papa, Christina, and Grant."

Will and Denielle greeted the adults and smiled shyly at the kids. The boy was about Christina's age, and the girl a little younger than Grant.

At first, there was an uncomfortable silence between the kids. Then remembering his manners, Will crossed his arms over his chest, and said, "We just got out of school for the summer."

"We did too," Christina said, fiddling with a pamphlet on the table.

Denielle looked at Grant shyly. "Are you two here for the tour?"

Before Grant could answer, Helene looked at her watch. "Well, I'm afraid you've missed the regular tour, but if you'd like, the children can take you around, and you can catch up with Gus and the others at the end. How does that sound?"

"Come on," Denielle pulled Christina by the hand. "Let's hurry. Gus is the most fun guide ever, and does the coolest tours!"

"Yeah," Will said, "let's go. My sister and I know about everything here. We can still catch up with Gus at the end. You won't want to miss it. It's the best part of the tour!"

"Can we go?" Christina asked. She and Grant looked hopefully at their grandparents.

"Sure, you kids go on ahead," Papa said. "We'll be here reminiscing with Ms. Helene until you get back." As the kids left the room, Papa began humming to the song currently playing over the loud speaker. "My girl," he sang to Mimi.

5

LIVING IN THE "D"

"So where are you guys from?" Will asked Christina as they walked down a long hall filled with pictures of Motown's legendary artists.

"Peachtree City, Georgia—near Atlanta," Christina told him proudly. "How about you?"

"Oh, we've been in the 'D' all our lives," Will said.

Christina gave him a puzzled look. "The 'D'? Where's that?"

"You know, 'D'—Detroit. Don't tell me you haven't heard that expression since you've been here," he said.

Christina flipped her stick-straight brown hair back over her shoulders. "Well, we just got here today," she said.

"But we've been here long enough to hear about a mystery already!" Grant piped in.

That got Will's attention. "What are you talking about?" he asked.

Grant explained how they had met Mr. Joe at the Yankee Air Museum, and how Gus had mentioned the eerie noises in the basement to him.

Will shrugged. "Yeah, I suppose it could be called a mystery," he said. "I overheard my grandmother talking to Gus about it the other day. Something about the neighbors calling because of strange noises coming from the basement late at night. But Mr. Tom, our night watchman, claims he doesn't know what they're talking about. I'd sure like to find out what's going on, but I don't want to bother my grandmother with it right now. She has enough on her mind with the Motown Review coming in two days."

"So, what if we help you solve the mystery for her?" Grant suggested.

Christina threw up her hands. "Well, here we go again," she told Grant. "How do we always end up getting involved in a mystery wherever we go?"

Grant rubbed his hands together and smiled. "Just lucky, I guess."

6
I HEARD IT THROUGH THE GRAPEVINE

Grant and Christina were disappointed at first as they looked at the pictures hanging around the museum. They had never heard of any of the artists displayed on the walls. In fact, they had never even seen a real record. It showed on their faces.

Will knew that a lot of kids who came to the museum felt the same way at first. That's why Gus worked so hard to make it a fun experience for them, and to teach them the Temptation Walk, made famous by The Temptations singing group. It helped kids to share the joy of the Motown music. It didn't matter if they knew who the singers were or not.

Will pointed to a picture on the wall. "This is Berry Gordy, Jr. who started Motown in 1959," he explained. "He purchased this house and used it for his small record company and his home. He was the first African American to blend rhythm and blues with certain elements of pop music. He created a new musical culture called 'soul' for African American singers. He helped shape one of the most incredible cultural periods in Detroit history!"

Will led the kids to a glass case. "Here's a group you might recognize. It's the Jackson Five." As the kids peered over the glass, he said, "Look at the youngest boy in the group. That's Michael Jackson."

"Wow!" said Grant. "Now that's someone I've heard of!"

"Yes," Christina agreed. "He was amazing!" She strolled along the long glass cases to examine more Jackson Five memorabilia. "Just look at all this stuff!"

Christina was entranced by elaborate stage outfits from The Jackson Five, sparkling jewelry, concert tickets, and the red leather jacket worn by Michael Jackson in a famous music video. She suddenly stopped short.

"Grant!" she cried. "Look at this! It's Michael Jackson's crystal-beaded glove!"

Grant's blue eyes grew wide. "Are those stones real?" he asked. Christina nodded, not taking her eyes off the sparkling glove.

Other cases held pieces of precious clothing like a beaded dress Diana Ross wore on one of her tours, a glittering dinner jacket worn by Smokey Robinson, and one of the famous gold tuxedos of The Temptations music group.

"Those guys sure knew how to dress!" Grant exclaimed. "Shiny and sparkly and really cool!"

Will smiled and led them into Studio "A" where the Motown hits of the 1960s and 70s were recorded. A piano, drum set, and microphones sat in the same places as they did when Motown legends filled the room.

Grant stepped up to the microphone and started singing. "I heard it through the grapevine!" he bellowed out. He snapped his fingers to the left, rolled his hands, then snapped his fingers to the right.

Will, Christina, and Denielle's incredulous stares made Grant giggle. "What?" he asked. "I know that song playing over the loudspeaker. It's the dancing raisin song, right? I'm doing the raisin dance." He finished with a big spin, and bowed. "So, what do you think?" he asked the kids.

Denielle put her hand over her mouth and giggled. "Oh, Grant, you are sooo silly!"

Grant tipped the microphone stand and spoke into it. "Well, thank you, thank you very much!" he said in a low voice.

"Don't encourage him," Christina whispered in Denielle's ear, loud enough for Grant to hear. "He'll just start showing off and embarrass us."

"I heard that," Grant said, making a face at his sister.

Will looked at his watch. "OK you guys, let's head upstairs to the echo chamber. We should be able to catch up with Gus after that."

He stopped just outside the door of the echo chamber. "This room helped create an echo effect or 'reverb' to a voice during a song," Will explained. He led them inside and pointed to a square cut into the ceiling. "This opening helped make the sound bigger."

"Watch this," Denielle said. She clapped her hands with a loud SMACK! The sound vibrated throughout the room.

"Waayyy cool!" Grant said. "Let me try." He cupped his hands around his mouth and sang, "Day-O, D-A-A-A-Y-O!"

They all put their hands over their ears. "OK, Grant, we get the picture!" Christina hollered through his echoes.

7
MISSING MUSIC

The kids finally caught up with Gus and his tour group. Gus was very tall, with salt and pepper hair and brown eyes that twinkled with merriment when he talked about the years of Motown music. He pumped the crowd full of interesting details and fun facts, and they loved him.

Will waved at Gus. He waved back and held up a finger to signal that he'd still be a while.

Gus held the crowd captivated. "How many times in your life will you get to stand in the exact spot as some of Motown's most famous musicians?" he asked. "You are literally standing where Smokey Robinson, Marvin Gaye, The Temptations, The Four

Tops, and Diana Ross and The Supremes recorded their hits. Isn't that incredible?" The crowd applauded in response.

As they watched Gus charm his audience, Will turned to Christina. "My grandmother told me that old Gus used to be a singer and wanted to work for Motown Records. He'd written a wonderful song, hired an agent over the phone, and mailed him a piece of paper with the lyrics and melody on it. Gus had even made up dance steps to go along with the song. Dance steps were a big part of the Motown sound," he explained. "The agent said he'd get back to Gus and when he did, he **rebuffed** the idea and told Gus that the song was no good. Gus was very disappointed. He thought he had written a song worthy of the Motown label."

"Gosh, that's terrible!" Christina said. "What happened?"

Will glanced at Gus. "A few months after he had been told the bad news, another band released a song with the same melody as the one Gus wrote. They were not a Motown group. They were from another record company. The lyrics were different, but the music was definitely the same."

"But what happened to the original song sheet Gus wrote?" asked Grant.

Will shrugged. "That's the strangest thing. It disappeared too. The agent denied ever seeing the paper with the melody and words on it. My grandmother said when he did that he **impugned** Gus's character. And, it was his word against Gus's that it even existed."

"So what happened then?" Christina asked.

"Gus refused to ever sing his song again," Will said. "Sometimes he'll hum the melody, but I've never heard him sing the words. He says he's happy just working here and being around the music industry he loved so much."

"Do you know the melody to the song?" Grant asked.

"Sure. It goes like this..." Will hummed the tune.

"Hmmm, that song sounds familiar, but I can't quite put my finger on it," Grant said.

He started humming it too. Maybe he'd heard Mimi and Papa singing it in the car. They were always singing old songs while they drove on trips.

The kids stood with the crowd and watched Gus conduct the last part of the tour. Will and Denielle had stepped away to speak to someone they knew.

"PSSSSTTT..." Grant tugged on Christina's arm.

"What?" Christina leaned down to listen.

Grant spoke close to her ear. "I want to have a look in the basement."

"And just how are you supposed to break away to do that?" she whispered.

Grant smiled. "I'll tell Will that I have to use the bathroom. And, actually, I really do!"

Christina smiled. "Why am I not surprised?" she asked. She tapped her cheek. "Actually, that's waaaay believable! Let's go tell him."

They ran up behind an alcove where Will was speaking to a tall, husky man with a thick, black mustache. They didn't want to be rude and interrupt, so they stayed back. As they waited, they couldn't help but overhear the last part of their conversation. The man shook his finger at Will.

"OK, Mr. Tom, we'll stay out of the basement," Will said.

"Did you hear that?" Grant whispered to Christina. "It's Mr. Tom, the guy Mr. Joe told us about! He looks mad, and he definitely doesn't want us going near the basement."

"Then go quickly while he's still talking to Will," said Christina. "And Grant, don't get lost, don't get into any trouble, and don't stay away too long."

Will and Denielle came back over to Christina and Grant. "My brother needs to go to the bathroom," Christina said. "Is there one near here?"

"There is a restroom. It's near the basement," Will replied. "I'll take you, Grant."

Grant gave him a dismissive flick of his hand. "No need. I can find it by myself." *Their plan had worked perfectly*, Grant thought, as he started to walk away.

Christina looked over her shoulder. "Remember what I said, Grant."

Suddenly, Christina shivered. *Something just doesn't feel right*, she thought.

8
A SECRET COMPARTMENT

Grant found the stairs that led to the basement. He glanced around, and seeing no one to stop him, started down the creaky steps. *It's very quiet, and maybe a little creepy,* he thought. He started whistling the tune Will had hummed for them. At the bottom of the steps, he turned right and entered a narrow hallway.

When he came to a door marked STORAGE, Grant turned the doorknob. *I wonder what's in here?* he thought. *Ghosts, probably*, his subconscious mind piped in before he could stop it. He nervously hummed the tune this time to shake off the fear. "Oh well, ghosts or no ghosts, I'm still a super snooper," he whispered out loud.

The room was silent, and smelled of dust and old age. Wooden tables and chairs were stacked in a corner. A pile of old posters and pictures leaned against the wall. Nothing seemed amiss.

As Grant moved further into the room, he noticed that it was L-shaped, so that the other part of the room was not visible from the doorway. When he made the turn, he spied scrapes and gouge marks all over the floor, like someone had been dragging furniture across it. The deepest scrapes led to an old desk sitting way back in a corner, but several boxes were strewn around the floor, blocking it in.

Someone had been down here, and it was definitely not a ghost. *This place is a mess*, Grant thought. *But what were they looking for? And if Mr. Tom had really checked this place out, surely he would have seen all those scrapes.* Grant hummed the tune again as he shoved the boxes out of the way, cutting a path to the desk.

A thick layer of dust covered the desk. It looked pretty rickety. One of its legs was broken and propped up with an old tin can, but at one time it must have been beautiful. Grant touched one of the drawer pulls. It was a small gold lion's head. "Whoaaa, that's awesome!" he said.

He sat in the wobbly green chair in front of the desk. When he swiveled, it squeaked. Grant pulled the top right drawer open. It was empty except for a lone paperclip. Then he pulled on the center drawer. It held a few random pens and pencils in the built-in tray, but the rest of the drawer seemed to be empty. "Too bad. Nothin' cool here," Grant said with disappointment.

But the drawer was deep, so he reached in further. As he felt around inside, something sharp scraped across the top of his hand.

"Ouch!" Grant jerked his hand out and licked the scrape on his knuckles to soothe them. Something was definitely in there, and being Grant, he wanted to see what it was.

This time when he stuck his hand back in, he was more careful. His fingertips brushed what felt like a small latch. He grasped it between his thumb and index finger, and gave it a tug. To his surprise, the lever moved and the bottom of the drawer popped up.

"Sweet!" Grant exclaimed. "A secret compartment!"

Grant peeked inside. There wasn't much room in there, but Grant could definitely see something that looked like a sheet of paper. He couldn't get it out with his hand. He opened another drawer looking for something to help him pull it out, and found a tarnished, silver letter opener. He gently poked it inside the secret compartment, and pulled on the paper with the flat side of the letter opener so he didn't tear it.

Inch by inch, he slid it out. His prize was a crinkled piece of paper, yellowed with age. When he looked closely, Grant saw that it had musical notes on it and the words to a song.

"Man, this is really old!" Grant exclaimed. He couldn't read music, but since the melody of the tune he had been humming was still playing in his head, he decided to put the lyrics on the paper to it. To his surprise, the lyrics fit the melody perfectly.

"Wow, I've gotta' show this to the others!" Grant cried. He ran up the stairs with the sheet music in his hand. When he reached the top, he carefully slid it into an inside pocket of his backpack so it wouldn't get crushed.

In his haste, Grant did not see the mysterious figure hiding by the stairwell, watching his every move.

9
PUT ON YOUR DANCIN' SHOES!

Grant reappeared just as Gus was finishing the tour, and tapped his sister on her shoulder. "Psssst, I'm back," he said.

"Do you realize how long you've been gone?" Christina asked. "I was worried I might have to tell Mimi and Papa that you were missing."

"Missing what?" Papa's booming voice rang out next to them. He, Mimi, and Helene had come to see the kids do the Temptation Walk dance routine. Papa was ready to dance himself.

"Ahhhh," Grant began, "we didn't want you to miss the Temptation Walk. I hear it's the best part of the tour!"

"Good one," Christina said under her breath and started to walk away.

"But wait!" Grant tugged on the sleeve of his sister's shirt. "Wait'll you see what I found!"

But she and the others were too excited about doing the Temptation Walk to listen. "Tell me later, Grant," Christina said over her shoulder as she hurried off.

Gus clapped his hands to get everyone's attention. "All right, let's get this party started!" he cried. The crowd cheered.

"Now, in addition to their sound," Gus added, "two of the key elements that distinguished the Motown artists from others were their uniquely polished style and fancy dance steps. The Temptation Walk was made famous by the music group The Temptations."

Gus arranged Christina, Grant, Will, and Denielle as the backup singers, and Papa as the lead singer in the group.

"OK, here we go!" Gus announced. "Follow me on three. One, two, three, go! Step, cross, step, cross, and dip," he instructed. "OK, now step, touch, step, touch, step, touch. All right! You're doing great! Now everybody scoop, scoop, scoop," he said, rocking his arms back and forth, "and that's the Temptation Walk!"

All the onlookers applauded and cheered.

Gus smiled. "Now let's put it to music. Everybody ready?"

"Whoooo-Hoooo!" Grant shouted. "Let's go!"

Papa gave a shrill whistle through his teeth. "Yeeee-Haaaa!"

Gus started the music. He led the kids and Papa through the steps again. This time, everyone put their all into it.

"Oh yeah, oh yeah, I'm feelin' it!" Grant said, flailing his arms in the air. Then, to show off, he decided to add a spin to the dance. But halfway though his spin, he tripped over his own feet, and tumbled to the ground. Laughter and applause bounced off the walls.

Christina laughed so hard that her blue eyes watered with tears. "Oh, yeah, little brother, you've got it all right," she said and gave him a hand up. They all thanked Gus for teaching them the Temptation Walk as Papa ushered them to the door.

As they headed for the exit, Papa held Grant's and Denielle's hands in his so they wouldn't get lost in the swarm of people around them. When they reached the front door, Grant tugged on Papa's sleeve. "Can Will and Denielle stay at the hotel and go sightseeing with us tomorrow?"

Papa ruffled Grant's hair. "Sure little partner, as long as their grandmother says it's OK."

Helene put her arms around the kids' shoulders. "Would you two like to go sightseeing with Christina and Grant?"

Denielle nodded vigorously, and Will shouted, "For real? Thanks, Grandma! I'll just run and pack our things."

Christina got caught in the crowd on the way out. She felt pushed and shoved from all sides. She finally stopped and leaned up against a wall to catch her breath.

Finally, with the last of the visitors gone, Christina was able to move again. As she started forward, she noticed a scrap of paper on the floor by her feet. She reached down and picked it up. It was another torn piece of a photograph. It looked like the legs of a pair of men's trousers. She slipped the torn picture into her purse.

"Wait until I show this to Grant!" she said, running to catch up with her family.

Papa hustled everyone to the waiting taxi. "Let's head 'em up and move 'em out to the hotel!" Mimi and the kids piled into the taxi, humming music from The Temptations.

No one saw a man jump into a gleaming black sedan and pull out behind their taxi.

10
LIVING LARGE!

The taxi rounded the corner of Jefferson Avenue, and they caught their first glimpse of the Detroit Renaissance Center. Made completely of reflective glass, the enormous skyscrapers shimmered in the late afternoon sun. Christina gasped. She had to crane her neck to see the Marriott Hotel spiking through the center of the other four buildings, dwarfing them.

"Wow!" Christina squealed. "I didn't know a hotel could be that tall!"

Soaring glass ceilings dominated the entrance of the building, and lush palm trees stood majestically in rows like giant guards keeping watch over a palace. Overstuffed burgundy, blue, and gold couches dotted the elegant lobby.

Grant plopped his backpack on the marble floor right where he stood, and just stared at everything around him. His eyes were drawn to the many escalators and odd little platforms and catwalks above and below each floor.

"Just look at this place!" cried a delighted Grant. "It's like a massive space station!"

Papa called the kids to join him at the reception desk. "Mimi was able to get us upgraded to the Henry Ford Suite," he told them. "We got a little help from Mr. Schema, the hotel manager, of course," he added, tipping his Stetson hat to the executive.

Papa handed a plastic key card to each child. "The suite has three bedrooms, so the boys will have their own room, and so will you girls."

"Yesssss!" Christina shouted. She was so happy not to have to share a room with her brother. He always dumped his backpack out on the bed, and she was forever stepping on his junk lying on the floor.

Then, Christina realized what Papa had just said. "Wait a minute, the Henry Ford Suite?" she asked. She looked at the hotel manager. "Did Henry Ford live here?"

Mr. Schema laughed. "No, miss. Henry Ford II enlisted the support of the Ford Motor Company and other Detroit businesses to build the Renaissance Center to help revive the downtown economy. The Henry Ford Suite was named in his honor."

A bellhop loaded their mounds of luggage onto a wheeled cart. Mimi always carried a lot of luggage when she traveled. She didn't go anywhere without her red suits, evening wear for her and Papa, high heels, laptop computer, research books, and camera.

Papa just shook his head as he always did when they traveled. They entered the glass elevator and the bellhop pushed the button to the 68th floor.

Grant looked down at the other towers surrounding the hotel. "The towers look like giant spaceships from here!"

The bellhop smiled. "The Renaissance Center is a group of interconnected skyscrapers. There's a shopping mall and a movie theater in that one," he said, pointing to one of the towers. "And if you want some exercise, you can walk eight times around the glass walkway that connects the four towers, and you'll have walked a mile."

At Grant's hopeful look, Mimi said, "I think we'll just pass on that one for now."

11
SWEET SUITE!

When the bellhop opened the door to their suite, Mimi gasped with delight.

Glittering gold chandelier light bathed the living room and dining room, and all the rooms had floor-to-ceiling windows that offered spectacular views of downtown Detroit and the Detroit River.

Mimi pointed to the shores of Canada just across the water. "Look, kids, that's Windsor, Ontario, over there. Imagine, being able to look into another country right out the window!"

"That's waaaayyyyy cool!" the kids all agreed.

"We need to get cleaned up and get these children to dinner," Mimi said. "And I have the perfect spot picked out right here in the hotel."

"How 'bout just an hour's shut eye for the old man?" Papa pleaded. His eyelids were already drooping.

Mimi gave in. "OK. I'll just jot down my notes from today and then freshen up."

"Bless you, ma'am," Papa said, kissing Mimi's hand.

The kids started to sneak down the hall. "Hold it right there," Mimi said, stopping them in their tracks. "You kids make sure you unpack your things neatly, and hang up your clothes."

"I hate to be neat," Grant grumbled, tugging his suitcase to his room.

Later, the kids gathered in Christina's room. Christina took the piece of torn photograph out of her purse. "Look what I found on the floor in the Motown Museum," she said. She showed it to the others. "Someone must've dropped it."

Grant saw what it was and gasped. "Oh my gosh!" he exclaimed.

"What?" Will asked, confused.

Grant handed the clue to Will, and he examined it. "It looks like a picture of a pair of men's trousers. How weird is that?" He handed it to Christina.

Christina turned it over and read the message.

> *He stood by while they did the deed.*

"What do you think it means?" Will asked.

Christina placed her hand on Will's arm. "It means we have a mystery to solve at the Motown Museum."

"I don't know if our grandmother would want us to solve a mystery," Denielle said.

Will looked at his sister. "Not now, Denielle," he said.

Will turned back to Christina. "Why?" he asked. "What possible connection can this torn photograph have with the mystery at the museum?"

Grant pulled the other piece of torn photograph out of his shirt pocket and waved it in front of Will's eyes. "Because we got one this morning just after we learned about the strange things going on in the basement at the museum!"

"But, Mr. Tom said there's nothing going on down there," Will said.

"Tell him, Grant," Christina urged.

"Well," Grant began. "Remember while we were waiting for Gus to teach us the Temptation Walk, and I went to the bathroom? I also went into the basement to see if there was actually something going on down there."

"I see," Will said, anger in his voice. "You just took it upon yourself to go and snoop in the basement?" He threw up his hands. "What if someone had been down there doing—who knows what? You could have been in real danger!"

"You don't know Grant," Christina cut in, defending her brother. "He's a super snooper, and very good about not getting caught."

Grant looked at Will. "The point is that I *did* go into the basement, and I discovered several suspicious looking scrapes on the floor, like someone's been dragging furniture around looking for something." He snapped his fingers as if a light bulb had gone off in his head. "Hey, wait a minute, I may know the answer to that—"

"Hey, kids, it's time to go to dinner!" Papa bellowed from the living room.

"Uh, oh, I think our hour is up," said Christina. "We'll have to talk more about this later. Papa doesn't like to wait!"

Grant started to run into his room to get his backpack. "But, Christina, I found..."

"Yo, let's get them doggies movin', nowwwww!" Papa howled.

Christina was already running down the hallway. "You can tell us later," she instructed over her shoulder. "It'll have to keep until then."

As they all hurried into the elevator, no one saw the man get off the other one, nodding his head as the elevator doors slowly closed.

12
A MOTOWN CITY OF LIGHTS

"How about taking the glass elevator up to the highest floor in the hotel to have dinner?" Papa suggested.

"Now that's what I'm talking about!" Grant exclaimed.

The family piled into the outside glass elevator. It slowly climbed up...up...up, giving them a magnificent view of the sparkling lights of downtown Detroit, Cobo Hall, and Hart Plaza. The Motor City spanned as far and wide as the eye could see.

The doors opened on the 72nd floor, and the group stepped out into an elegant restaurant. The hostess seated them next to tall windows offering a fabulous view of the Ambassador Bridge. Its lights shimmered in the distance.

Their waiter, Jordan, was fun and made the group feel welcome. He saw them gazing at the Ambassador Bridge. "Magnificent, isn't she? I work here every evening, and I never get tired of seeing her."

"Do you know a lot about the bridge, Jordan?" Mimi asked.

"Yes, ma'am," he said proudly. "Being from Detroit, we learned about the bridge in school. It's quite a wonder." He pointed out the window. "The Ambassador Bridge was constructed in 1929 to connect the United States to Canada. When it was built, it was the longest suspension bridge in the world!"

"That's very impressive," Papa commented.

Jordan snapped his fingers. "And did you know that there's also a tunnel you can drive through to get from Detroit to Canada?"

At their astonished looks, Jordan laughed. "It's true," he said. "It was built shortly after the Ambassador Bridge. Imagine driving in a partially submerged highway tunnel connecting Detroit to Windsor, Ontario!"

"That is wayyyyy cooollll!" Grant said. "Do you use the tunnel, too?"

Ice clinked in their glasses as Jordan filled them with water. "All the time, although I have to admit, it can be a little scary if you get stuck in traffic under there. You see, at its lowest point, the Detroit-Windsor Tunnel is about 75 feet below the surface of the Detroit River."

"Oh," Christina said, "I'm not sure I'd like that either! What if the tunnel sprung a leak?"

Grant's eyes grew wide. "I was just thinking the same thing," he said.

"OK," Papa cut in, "Let's order, and then let's eat!"

The group dined on cedar planked maple salmon, orange chicken, mashed potatoes, carrots, and creamed spinach.

"That meal was just about as good as the view," Papa announced. Grant and Christina nodded, their spoons furiously dipping in and out of creamy ice cream sundaes for dessert.

When Jordan brought the check, he suggested they walk around and enjoy the view. "If you look down from here, you'll see that all the roads leading out from the hotel look like the spokes of a gigantic wheel."

As they made their way to the elevator, Grant remembered that he had yet to tell Christina about the sheet music he had found. He just needed to find the right time.

13

THINGS THAT GO BUMP IN THE NIGHT

Something woke Christina and she sat straight up in her bed. "Listen, do you hear that?" she asked.

"Hear what?" Denielle replied in a groggy voice.

"Like something is scratching at our door," Christina said, flicking on her bedside lamp. "Listen, there it goes again."

Christina knew that Mimi and Papa were already asleep in another part of the suite. She pulled the covers up to her chin, and drew her knees up. What if it was a burglar?

She quietly tiptoed out of bed. Her hands were shaking. She needed protection, so she looked around for something she might use as a weapon.

Her water bottle sat on the nightstand beside her. *Hey, any weapon is better than none,* she thought. She grabbed the neck of the bottle like a club and tiptoed across the room. She raised the water bottle over her head, held her breath, and yanked the door open.

"Boo!" Grant's smiling face greeted her in the doorway.

Christina leaned against the wall, her heart pounding. "Why can't you just knock like everyone else?" she hissed.

Grant wiggled his fingers in front of her face. "What, were you scared?" he teased.

"You just made my heart stop is all," Christina said, clutching her chest. "Hi, Will," she added, waving a limp hand at him as he bounded into the bedroom behind Grant.

Denielle sat up in her bed, rubbing her eyes. "Is it morning?" she asked when she saw Grant and Will standing in their room.

"No, just some late-night fun, courtesy of my little brother," Christina said.

Christina crossed her arms over her chest and glared at Grant. "So, why have you come calling in the middle of the night?"

"Well," Grant began, "Will and I decided to sneak into the kitchen for a snack."

"Grant, we just had a huge dinner a few hours ago," Christina reminded him.

Grant smiled sheepishly. "Yeah, but that was grownup food. We wanted SNACKS!"

Christina rolled her eyes. "That's right, I forgot I was talking to the eating machine."

Grant plopped down on her bed. "Anyway," he said, "when we walked past the foyer on our way to the kitchen, there was a piece of paper lying on the floor just inside the door. Thinking it was a message from the hotel, I picked it up. And lookey, lookey what I found!" Grant waved a folded piece of paper in front of her face.

Christina snatched it away from him. As she unfolded it, the other kids gathered around her. The message read:

His raised hand could have righted a wrong.

And there, taped to the bottom of the note was another piece of the picture. It was part of a man's suit coat with his arm raised as if he were waving at someone.

Christina handed the piece of torn picture to Will. He turned it over a few times. "Another meaningless clue," he said, tossing it back at Christina.

Christina caught it and said, "Don't you see, Will? It's just like a scavenger hunt. You know, you get pieces of a puzzle and collect them until you solve the mystery. Let's put the three pieces of the picture together. If they fit, we'll know that they're from the same picture."

Christina took the other two photo pieces out of the drawer in her nightstand, laid them on her bed, and gently pushed them together. They fit seamlessly.

Will pointed to the three torn pieces. "What does that prove?"

Christina's head came up. "It proves that someone is trying to tell us something, that's what! These clues are connected as a whole even though they were found in three different locations."

"OK," Will grunted. "Let's just say for one nanosecond that I buy into this story. So, why doesn't this mystery person just walk up to us and tell us who they are and what they want? Why so mysterious?"

"I think this person wants to stay anonymous for some reason," Christina said. "Maybe..."

"THIS PARTY'S OVER!" Papa's voice boomed from the doorway.

"Oh, hi, Papa," Christina said pleasantly. "We were just..."

"Do you know what time it is? Papa bellowed. "We have a very full day tomorrow and have to get up in..." He looked at his watch. "Four hours! Now you kids drop what you're doing and skedaddle to bed."

He pointed to the two boys. "March!"

14
A BLAST FROM THE PAST

As the white tour bus pulled through the gates, the guide explained, "Greenfield Village is the largest indoor-outdoor museum complex in America." She pointed to several buildings on their right. "Henry Ford moved more than one hundred historical buildings to the property from their original locations, and arranged them in a village setting to show how Americans have lived and worked since the founding of our country."

She pointed to a tidy white house with black shutters. "That's Noah Webster's home, where he wrote the first American dictionary."

"Oh, look, there's the clock tower!" Mimi exclaimed, pointing to a brown brick building with a huge clock in the center of a tall steeple. "It's a replica of Independence Hall in Philadelphia, where the Declaration of Independence was signed."

Papa, Grant, and Will bounded off the bus as soon as it stopped to get a look at some new Ford Mustangs parked outside.

"Boys just love cars, don't they?" Denielle asked Mimi.

Mimi nodded. "Cars and airplanes and all kinds of expensive toys!" she replied.

The group entered the building where they met a young woman at the reception desk. "Welcome to Greenfield Village, we hope you enjoy your stay," she remarked. She smiled at Mimi. "Would you like a map, ma'am?"

"Yes, four please," said Mimi. She handed them out to the kids. "Just in case you get lost."

As the group studied the map of the layout of Greenfield Village, they all started talking at once. It seemed that everyone wanted to see and do something different. The kids wanted to go to the Henry Ford Museum and Mimi wanted to see Greenfield Village.

Papa silenced them by holding up his hand. "Let's not **quibble**," he said. "We'll take a quick trip through the village first and then visit the museum. How's that?"

Everyone agreed and followed Papa through the double doors that led to Greenfield Village.

Stepping out onto the sidewalk of Greenfield Village was like stepping back in time. An old Ford Model T car puttered down the street, while horse-drawn carriages clomped lazily up and down beside it.

Mimi looked at her map and pointed. "There's Cotswold Cottage, the oldest building in Greenfield Village," she said. "It was built around 1620, about the time the first settlers were coming to America!" The old stone cottage was surrounded by flower gardens bursting with color, and bright green ivy had inched its way up the worn stone exterior.

Mimi sighed. "It looks like it came right out of a painting!"

They stopped in at Thomas Edison's laboratory, and learned about the invention of the light bulb. "The museum even uses some of the light bulbs made from one of Edison's designs," their guide explained.

Around the bend was the Firestone farm, where the group learned how people prepared and preserved foods in the past. "Firestone? As in the racing tires?" Grant asked the lady in the green skirt and hood giving them the tour.

"Yes, that Firestone," she said. "His family had a working farm in the mid 1800s."

Mimi knew time was running short. "You have to promise me, Papa," she said, "that we come back here later. I didn't get to shop, or see the Wright Brothers' Bicycle Shop, or ride the carousel, or take a test drive in the Model T, or..."

Papa stopped her short. "I get it, I get it," he said, smiling. "We'll be back, Greenfield Village!"

15
AUTHENTIC AUTOS

The Henry Ford Museum was housed in one of the old Ford factory buildings. Its high, domed ceilings and old wooden benches made it look like an old train station. Railroad tracks, once used to deliver coal and other supplies to the factory, ran down the center of the wooden floor.

For the next hour the group admired cars from the past, present, and future. After that, they studied the map more closely, and discovered that the museum had many other things to see and do. As they entered a long corridor, Grant gasped. "Ah, Papa," Grant whispered, pointing high above his head. "There's an airplane hanging from the ceiling."

Papa chuckled. "So there is," he said, ruffling Grant's hair.

"Hope it's tied up there really tight!" Grant exclaimed.

They moved from room to room. Papa pointed out a huge, original McDonald's hamburger sign boasting "Over 160 million sold." Grant and Christina were fascinated by the locomotives, historic airplanes, and rare vehicles on display—like the Oscar Mayer Wienermobile, a giant, red hot dog attached to the body of a car.

"I want to ride in that!" Grant said as he pointed and laughed. "Oh, I wish I were an Oscar Mayer Wiener," he sang along with the song playing at the exhibit. Christina joined in.

The kids became more serious at the next few exhibits. "Wow, look at this," Christina said in a solemn tone. She was gazing at a rocking chair from Ford's Theatre in Washington, D.C. "President Abraham Lincoln sat in that chair when he was shot in 1865," she said.

They moved to another area where Mimi walked up to a shiny black limousine. "That, children," she explained, "is the car

President John F. Kennedy was riding in when he was assassinated in Dallas, Texas, in 1963."

Christina gasped. "That's really the one?" she asked.

"Absolutely," Papa replied. "It was impounded for evidence after the assassination, but later modified and returned to service."

Will looked solemn as they approached a shiny, yellow and green bus with a white top.

"What's so special about a bus?" Grant asked as the kids stepped into the vehicle.

"A lady named Rosa Parks did something famous on this bus," Will explained. "In 1959, she refused to give up her seat to a white person and move to the back of the bus. African Americans were expected to ride in the back of the bus in those days in Montgomery, Alabama."

"I remember her!" Christina said, running her hands along the green vinyl seats. "We studied about her during Black History Week. She was arrested for violating segregation laws. After her arrest, local civil rights leaders got together and urged African Americans to stop riding all the city buses."

As they stepped off the bus, Will said, "The bus boycott was led by Dr. Martin Luther King, Jr. Rosa's case went all the way to the Supreme Court. They ruled that the segregation laws in Alabama were unconstitutional."

Will pointed at Rosa Parks's picture by the display. "She inspired others to fight for their civil rights, which started a new era for all African Americans," he said. "She was a great lady. There's even a street named after her in Detroit."

"Wow!" Christina said. "How cool is that?!"

"Speaking of cool," Grant said, "I'm thirsty and hungry! Are they selling any wieners at the wienermobile?"

Papa laughed. "No wieners there, but here's some money to get some vittles for you hungry young 'uns."

The kids quickly bought hot dogs and drinks and crowded around a table to eat.

Mimi and Papa wanted to linger a while longer at the exhibits, so they left the kids with a lecture.

"Everyone stay together," Papa said, looking straight at Grant. "And keep a close eye on Denielle." He looked at his watch. "Everyone meets by the reception area in a half-hour so we can go on the Ford Rouge Plant tour together. Agreed?"

"Agreed!" shouted the kids.

While they ate, the kids talked about the clues they had received.

Christina recapped the events by counting on her fingers. "Number one: we know Gus mailed his agent the song and it went missing. Two: we know someone is looking for something in the basement of the Motown Museum. And three: someone is sending us clues. I think there's a connection between the three."

"Like what?" Will asked.

Christina threw up her hands. "I have absolutely no idea."

That made Will smile. "Wouldn't it be cool if Gus could sing his song at the Motown

Review tomorrow night? That's where he wanted his song to be, after all." He put his chin in his hands and leaned his elbows on the table. "That is, if we could find it."

While he listened, Grant played sipping games with his straw. He stopped short when Will mentioned finding Gus's song. He leaped to his feet. "That's what I keep trying to tell you guys, I think I have the..."

Just as Grant was about to explain that he thought he had the original sheet music, the lid popped off his cup. His soft drink and ice cubes sloshed over the side, spilling down his arm and hand.

"WHOAAAAA!" Grant cried. As he tried to move away from the mess, he slipped on some ice on the floor. The cup went flying, spraying his hair, the table, and the floor.

"Oh no!" Christina cried, leaping forward to help him.

Will slid out of his chair and began mopping the sticky, slushy beverage from the table and floor. He tossed Christina some napkins to help mop up Grant.

Looking around at the disaster, Christina sighed. "Come on Grant, let's find a restroom where you can clean up before we meet Mimi and Papa."

Christina studied the map. "The restroom is just up ahead," she remarked. But suddenly, she caught a movement out of the corner of her eye. *Is that Mr. Tom watching us?* she wondered. She whirled around, but the man she saw had vanished into the group of people filing into the IMAX theatre.

16
A CLUE IN THE SHOE

Grant tugged on Christina's arm. "Come on," he pleaded. "I've gotta get this stuff out of my hair."

Christina told him she thought she'd seen Mr. Tom. "I'm almost sure it was him," she said. She nodded towards the restroom. "Hurry up in there so we can get back to the others."

When Christina and Grant returned to their table, she told Will who she thought she'd seen.

Will looked surprised. "Why would Mr. Tom want to follow us?"

Grant was beginning to think he knew the answer to that question. "Maybe it's because he knows I have the..."

Christina looked at her watch. "Time to go!" she announced. She took one last look around to make sure they had cleaned up everything. She spotted something under a table and called to her brother. "Grant, is that your shoe under that table?"

Grant looked down at his shoeless foot. Will and Denielle giggled. "Oops, almost forgot it!" he said. As he bent down to pick it up, he spied a scrap of paper inside it. "Oh my gosh!"

"What now?" Christina asked impatiently.

Grant waved the piece of paper. "Look, it's another clue!"

As before, it was a piece of a picture. This piece showed another arm and hand in a man's suit coat. On the back it said:

Instead, he let them steal the song.

"Wow," said Christina. "We'll put it with the others when we get back." She quickly tucked the picture into her purse.

As they scampered off, no one saw the man step out from behind the potted plants near where they had been sitting.

17
NOT YOUR AVERAGE FACTORY

"All aboard!" the driver of the Ford tour bus announced. The group boarded behind some other tourists for the fifteen-minute ride to the place where new Ford F150 trucks were assembled.

Through the miles of fences surrounding the area, the kids got their first look at the enormous factory that was the Ford Rouge Plant. Its massive silver smokestacks rose like giant missiles against the blue sky.

Christina pressed her face up against the window of the bus. "Look!" she cried. "It kind of looks like a small city!"

A tour guide was waiting for them at the entrance. She told them her name was

Samantha, and that she would be happy to answer any questions they might have.

"Please follow me to our Art of Manufacturing Theatre," Samantha said. "Take your seats quickly, so we can present a short film about the history of the plant."

Grant tossed his backpack on the seat next to him and leaned toward Christina. "Hey, this place is really cool! It looks just like a regular movie theatre. Where's the popcorn?"

"Shhhhh, Grant," Christina said.

The lights dimmed and the movie began. "The original Ford Rouge Plant was a city without residents," the film narrator said, "and the largest single industrial complex in the world. The factory had its own fire department, police force, and a fully staffed hospital. Its power plant produced enough electricity to light a city the size of nearby Detroit."

"Seriously?" Papa whispered to Mimi. "That's one powerful power plant!"

The movie showed people in fast motion working on the assembly line. "By the 1930s," the narrator said, "more than 100,000 people worked at the Rouge Plant. The plant made its own steel to make the automobiles, and had its own glass factory for the windshields and windows. Henry Ford's vision was to achieve a continuous manufacturing process from start to finish, starting with raw materials and ending with the completed product."

An aerial view of the Rouge Plant appeared. "The complex included ninety-three buildings," the narrator continued, "including a tire-making plant, engine plant, frame and assembly plant, transmission plant, radiator plant, and a tool and die plant."

"Wooooo, Wooooo!!!" Grant and Christina plugged their ears as a train whistle screeched. "The Rouge Plant had its own railroad with one hundred miles of track and sixteen locomotives."

The movie panned over the assembly line, and car engines roared in the background. VROOOMMM!! VROOOMMM!! Grant stuck his fingers in his ears, opened his mouth wide, and blinked rapidly at Christina.

Christina just shook her head at him. "I'm trying to watch a movie here," she whispered.

The narrator continued, "And one new car rolled off the line every forty-nine seconds."

"Wow!" Grant whispered to Will. "They really made them that fast?"

"Sure did!" Will replied.

When the lights came up, Samantha asked that everyone exit from the theatre so they could continue to the observation deck to see the living roof exhibit.

Grant started out of the aisle behind Will. "Oops, I forgot my backpack," he said and skipped back to his seat. There was no one else in the theatre. He grabbed his backpack but suddenly felt a presence behind him. He spun around and came face-to-face with Mr. Tom!

"Hey kid, I want to talk to you!" Mr. Tom's **raucous** voice penetrated the silence. He lunged for Grant's backpack over the seat, but Grant was quicker. He dashed through the door into the hallway.

Christina and Will were standing just outside the theatre door. "What took you so long?" Christina asked. "Mimi, Papa, and Denielle have already gone upstairs."

"Quick, start running!" Grant shouted, yanking her arm. "Mr. Tom's in there and he tried to grab my backpack!"

"Why would he want your backpack?" Will asked as they ran.

Grant was positive he knew the answer to that question now. "It's because he knows I have the..."

"Hey! You kids come back here!" Mr. Tom cried. He was gaining on them!

"Run faster!" Christina shouted. "We have to catch up with Mimi and Papa! Get on the elevator—NOW!"

The kids got to the elevator just as the doors closed.

"What do we do now?" Will asked.

"Quick—the stairs!" Grant shouted.

Mr. Tom's pounding footsteps got closer and closer. Grant and Will pushed the door open, and leaped up the stairs two at a time.

"Hey, slow down, you two!" Christina cried. Puffing and out of breath, she clung to the rail. "I'd like to still be breathing when we get there!" She continued to climb, but kept looking back to see if Mr. Tom had followed them into the stairwell.

18
A LIVING ROOF

The kids bolted through the door at the top of the stairs. Papa saw their red faces and chuckled. "Been running a marathon?"

"Oh, no, we just took the stairs," Christina panted, scanning all the faces in the crowd. Luckily, there was no sign of Mr. Tom. Christina, Grant, and Will stuck like glue to Mimi and Papa after that.

The kids stepped up to the protective glass overlooking a huge expanse of green plants growing on the roof. Christina gasped in surprise. "This is amazing," she said.

Their guide Samantha spoke. "Of all the innovations coming out of the newly restored Ford Rouge Center, none has attracted more interest than this living roof.

At 454,000 square feet, or roughly 10.4 acres, it is the largest living roof in the world."

Grant raised his hand. "Miss Samantha, why would anyone want to grow plants on the roof of a building?"

Samantha smiled. "That's a very good question," she said. "The living roof reduces the 'heat effect' created by the acres of tarred and paved surfaces here. It also insulates the building, which reduces our heating and cooling costs by up to five percent."

She waved her arm at the green expanse before them. "This living roof is planted with sedum, which is a type of groundcover. It traps airborne dust and dirt, absorbs carbon dioxide, and creates oxygen. All those things improve air quality."

Samantha smiled. "The living roof also creates a habitat for birds, butterflies, and insects."

"There are almost no words to describe this," Mimi said. "This is the most remarkable use of natural resources I have ever seen!"

Papa was impressed too. He turned to the kids. "I hope you all understand the importance of what you've just learned, because as more companies 'go green,' projects like this will play a big part in your future."

"I like it!" Grant said. "When we get back home, I'm going to ask my dad if I can grow stuff on the roof of our house too!"

"That concludes this part of our tour," Samantha said. "Please join me now as we visit the assembly line to watch how the F150 Ford trucks are made."

As they started to leave, Christina scanned the crowd again. *Is Mr. Tom up here?* she wondered. She had a feeling someone was watching them.

19
KEEP THE LINE MOVING!

Papa, Mimi, and the kids walked single file on the catwalk built around the perimeter of the assembly line. The popping and hissing of the welding robots could be heard behind the protective glass. The conveyor that moved the car pieces along looked like a slow-moving rollercoaster.

"Boy, I'd love to climb down there and ride that conveyor!" Grant exclaimed.

"I'm sure glad there's a glass wall between you and that factory," Mimi said, smiling at Grant, whose blue eyes were glued to the activity below him.

Papa pointed to his pamphlet. "It says here that the original Rouge Plant was a mile-and-a-half wide and more than a mile long. The floor area was crisscrossed by 120 miles of conveyors."

The platform holding them was quite high. Christina did not like heights, so she stayed as close to the wall as she could and scooted forward just enough to see over the railing. Different colored Ford F150 frames advanced down the assembly line, their doors following right behind them. They were assembled one after another, and moved along on a floor conveyor until they were completed.

"Would you look at that!" Papa exclaimed. He pointed as articulated arms helped a worker move and set a huge engine into place. "I could use one of those at home!"

Samantha heard Papa and explained what was happening. "The number one priority here," she said, "is keeping the assembly line moving." They watched as one of the workers drove a gleaming red truck, fully assembled, off the assembly line. "You know, before Henry Ford invented the assembly line, it took more than ninety hours to assemble one car. Now, more than one thousand trucks can be produced in a day!"

The tour was finished, and Papa rounded everyone up for the ride back to the hotel. "I hope you kids had a good time here today," he said. "This car company started with one man's dream. What you've seen today is a valuable lesson in what can be accomplished by following your dreams and setting big goals for yourself."

My goal for today, Christina thought, *is to find out what is going on, and why we're in the middle of it!*

20

SAY OPA!!

"Oh, here comes the People Mover!" Christina said, clapping her hands. Mimi, Papa, and the kids stood in Detroit's Renaissance Center terminal waiting for the automated rail transportation system to take them to Greektown for dinner. The terminal was deserted except for a man sleeping on a bench with a newspaper over his face.

The kids watched as the bobbing headlight of a silver twin-train rounded a curve and zoomed towards them.

WHOOOSH! The People Mover came to a smooth stop in front of them and the doors slid open. Grant and Will jockeyed for position to see who could get on first. Bright overhead lights illuminated a narrow aisle with rows of blue vinyl seats on either side.

As the People Mover zipped out of the station, the kids were surprised at how high up they were. "Look, we're above all the traffic!" Grant shouted. "Like flying in the sky!" He pumped his fist in the air. "Greektown, here we come!"

The People Mover stopped at the Greektown Station. A vivid display of multicolored neon lights stretched across the sides and windows of the station, then arched across the guideway.

"Wow! These lights are awesome!" Grant exclaimed, as he twirled to follow the lines of mesmerizing neon. Suddenly, he swayed. "Whoa, I feel like I'm floating," he said.

In Greektown, music and laughter filled the air, and the aroma of mouth-watering meats and spices reminded everyone that they were very, very hungry.

As they walked up the street, bakery windows tempted them with baklava and other delicious pastries. "Greektown is a historic area of Detroit," Mimi told them. "Some of the restaurants here date back to the early 1900s."

"So, where are we going for dinner, Papa?" Grant asked.

"Right here!" Papa said, leading the group into the Pegasus restaurant. Grant looked up at a bright neon sign showing a girl riding the mythical white horse, Pegasus.

Inside the restaurant, people chattered and dishes clanked. A waiter in a white shirt and black tie showed them to their table and handed them their menus.

"This menu's five pages long, and I don't even know what half this stuff is," Grant complained. "Maybe they have a kids' menu with hot dogs or something."

"It's Greek food, Grant, and it is very good," Mimi told him. "If you'd like, I can recommend a few things you kids might like."

All of the kids nodded in agreement.

When the waiter returned with their drink orders, Papa ordered saganaki as an appetizer.

"What is a soggy nokky?" Grant asked.

"It's flaming goat cheese, a tradition here in Greektown," Papa said. "Try it, you'll like it." Papa grinned when he heard the familiar sizzle of the cheese coming out of the kitchen. "Ah, here it is now!"

A waiter held a tray containing a square piece of fried cheese. While the group watched, he poured brandy over the cheese and lit it on fire.

"OPA!" he yelled. The flame shot up over a foot in the air, making everyone flinch. After a few seconds, he squirted lemon juice over it, and the flame died out. Papa took a knife, spread some of the hot cheese on a thick slice of Greek bread, and handed it to Grant.

Grant took a tentative bite. His eyes grew wide. "Yummmmy!" he shouted. He took another bite and giggled as a string of cheese drooped from the bread to his mouth.

Their food arrived soon after. Mimi had ordered a Greek salad for her and Papa, and the kids dove into the sampler platter of lamb, rice, stuffed grape leaves, and baked eggplant. When they finished, they piled into the People Mover and headed back to the hotel.

The group was quiet and sleepy after their long day. Grant started to stretch out on his seat when he noticed a piece of paper in the corner next to the wall.

"It can't be," Grant said. He grabbed it and ran back to where Christina was sitting.

She was half asleep with her eyes closed when Grant slid next to her and blew into her ear.

Christina opened one eye. "Grant, tell me you did not just blow into my ear," she whispered angrily. "I'll just close my eyes again until I wake from this terrible nightmare I'm having."

"I was just trying to get you to wake up," Grant said.

"Well, you were successful," Christina said. "So what do you want?"

"I just found another clue," Grant whispered, waving a piece of paper under her nose.

Christina rubbed her eyes. "Where did you find it?"

Grant motioned with his head. "On the back seat over there."

"OK, this is really starting to get creepy," she said. "Let me see it."

Like before, it was a piece of a photograph. This piece showed a man's chest in a suit coat. The words on the back said:

He never got it off his chest. Find the next clue and you'll learn all the rest.

The People Mover glided to a stop.

"We'll have to talk about this later," Christina whispered. But when they returned to their suite, Papa ordered everyone to bed.

Christina carefully dropped the five pieces of the photograph into her nightstand drawer. She turned out the lights, and fell into a fitful sleep. She dreamed of being chased by a faceless man wearing a suit.

21
THE "WHO" OF THE CLUES!

When the kids woke the next morning, they found a note on the kitchen table telling them that Mimi and Papa were out helping Helene run errands for the Motown Review.

Christina grabbed the pieces of paper and spread them out on the table. She and Denielle carefully taped the pieces of the torn picture together, while the boys wrote down all of the verses:

> *He walked away from someone in need.*
> *He stood by while they did the deed.*
> *His raised hand could have righted a wrong.*
> *Instead, he let them steal the song.*
> *He never got it off his chest. Find the next clue and you'll learn all the rest.*

The kids stared at the words. "What do you think it all means?" Will asked.

"I think someone is trying to tell us who took Gus's song!" Christina said. "Now, we just have to wait until we get the next clue to put it all together."

DING DONG! "Don't answer that doorbell," Christina said nervously. "There's no one home with us, and it could be Mr. Tom." She was still frightened from yesterday's close call.

They waited...but there was no sound from outside the door. Christina put her ear against it, but didn't hear anything.

Will looked through the peephole. "No one there," he announced.

"It could be a trick," Grant said.

Denielle folded her hands across her chest. "I'm scared," she said.

Will took her hand. "It's OK. Someone is probably playing a game with us," he reassured her.

They waited for a few more minutes. "I think the coast is clear," Grant said. "I say we open the door together and see what's out there."

The kids gathered their courage. Grant put his hand on the latch. "OK; I open it on three. One, two, threeeeee!"

Nothing was outside but a folded piece of paper.

Christina picked up the paper and glanced both ways down the hall. She pulled everyone back inside and locked the door.

"What does it say?" Will asked.

You know the man who wrote the song, and here's the man who did him wrong!

A piece of a picture fell out from the folded note. There, smiling back at them was the face of Mr. Tom!

The kids took the picture over to the table and attached it to the rest of the pieces they had taped together.

Will pointed to the full picture. "Mr. Tom is much younger and thinner here in this picture, but I would recognize that mustache anywhere!"

Christina looked at the others. "So, now we finally know that Mr. Tom stole Gus's song, but what does that have to do with us?" she asked. "Mr. Tom was after Grant's backpack for some reason."

Grant jumped up from his chair. "Because I have what he wants!" he shouted. Christina, Will, and Denielle looked at him as if he'd grown two heads.

"That's what I keep trying to tell you!" Grant said. "I think I have the original sheet music that Gus wrote!" He quickly recapped his adventure at the Motown Museum. "I found it in a hidden compartment in an old desk," he added.

"What?!" Christina grabbed Grant's shoulders. "You've had the original sheet music all this time?"

Grant shrugged. "Well, I did keep trying to tell you!"

"Where is it?" Christina asked.

"It's right here safe and sound in my backpack," Grant said proudly. He reached into an inner compartment and carefully pulled out the sheet music.

Christina was speechless as she gazed at the paper.

Grant quickly explained. "When I found it, I was humming the melody Will had told us was Gus's original song, and the words fit perfectly. I just know this is his song!"

The notes and words had faded some, so Christina held the sheet music up to the light to see it better. Will stood next to her.

"Oh, my gosh, it's real!" Will shouted. "It's Gus's song! Wait until he sees this!"

Suddenly, they heard Mimi, Papa, and Helene outside in the hall talking. Christina gathered everything into a pile.

"Hurry, let's get this stuff picked up quick!" she said. She shoved everything into Grant's backpack and tossed it to him.

22
A SCARY ENCOUNTER!

Papa paced the floor in his black tuxedo. "Hurry up, you slowpokes! We're going to be late for the dinner before the Motown Review. Helene is waiting for us in the Ambassador Ballroom!"

Mimi looked glamorous in her dark red chiffon dress that sparkled in the lights whenever she moved. Papa gave a low whistle as she twirled around in a slow circle.

Papa looked at his watch again. "Let's head 'em up and move 'em out!" he bellowed.

Christina, Grant, Will, and Denielle came running. Mimi straightened Grant's tie and clapped her hands in delight. "My, you all look so wonderful!" she exclaimed.

The hallway was crowded with people waiting to get on the elevator for the evening's festivities. "DING!" The elevator bell signaled and the doors opened.

Oh snap! I forgot my backpack with the sheet music in it! Grant thought. While Mimi, Papa, and the other kids got on the elevator, he ran back to their suite.

Grant put his key card in the door slot. He heard the click, click of the electronic lock give way and hurried inside. He ran down the hall to his room and pulled his backpack out from under the bed. When he raced back into the hallway, he didn't see anyone familiar.

"Where is Grant?" Papa asked in the lobby.

Christina looked around. "I don't know. He was right behind me when we were getting on."

"Dagnabit!" Papa bellowed, swatting his knee with his cowboy hat. "We're late. How in the world did Grant get away without us seeing him?"

Mimi touched his hand. "Why don't we go on ahead?" she suggested. "The kids can wait for Grant right here."

Papa looked at his watch. They were already terribly late. "OK, but you kids stay together and come straight to the Ambassador Ballroom in the West Tower."

"We will," Christina assured him.

When Grant stepped out of the elevator, Christina, Will, and Denielle were waiting for him. "You are soooooo in BIG trouble, little brother," Christina said. "Luckily, Mimi talked Papa into going on ahead."

Grant winced. "But I forgot my backpack," he said, patting its side.

Christina was already leading them across the lobby. "You'll have to explain that to Papa later," she remarked. They walked quickly to the West Tower and boarded the elevator. After gliding past a few floors, the elevator stopped.

Christina stifled a scream. Mr. Tom was getting on the elevator! Christina looked around, but there was no escape. She and the others huddled in the corner, hoping he wouldn't see them among the other people.

The floors ticked by as the elevator rose. Christina felt sweat bead up on her forehead. After what seemed like forever, the elevator finally stopped. As soon as the doors slid open, the kids raced out.

Mr. Tom saw them. "Hey! You kids! Stop!"

They ran full steam into the Ambassador Ballroom with Mr. Tom on their heels.

"Wait a minute!" Mr. Tom cried. "I want to talk to you!"

"Papa!" Christina shrieked his name as the kids barged into the ballroom.

Mr. Tom skidded to a halt as Papa stepped into his path and held up his hand. "I suggest you stop right there, partner," he said.

Mimi and Helene came quickly. "What is the meaning of this?" Helene said. "Let's go somewhere more private so we don't upset our guests."

She led them over to a table in the corner of the room. Christina noticed that Gus was sitting nearby with some of the men they had met at the Yankee Air Museum. They all stood as Papa ushered Mr. Tom to a chair.

Papa stared intently at Mr. Tom. "Start talking," he demanded.

23
A STARTLING CONFESSION

Christina peeked from behind Papa and took his hand. She felt a little safer with her grandfather standing next to her. She pointed at Mr. Tom. "Papa, that man stole Gus's song!"

"No, I..." Mr. Tom stammered, looking from Christina to Papa.

"What? I don't understand," Papa said.

"It's a long story," Christina said.

Papa crossed his arms over his chest and glared at Mr. Tom. "Well, I'd like to hear it."

The other kids gathered around Christina. "OK, Papa," she said. "We discovered that Mr. Tom stole a song Gus wrote a long time ago."

"Wait, that's not entirely true," Mr. Tom said, desperately trying to say something in his own defense.

"Grant found it hidden in an old desk," Christina explained. "When Mr. Tom discovered that Grant had it, he tried to get it from him by chasing us in the Rouge Plant."

Christina looked straight at Mr. Tom. "Why did you do it?" she demanded.

Mr. Tom looked from Papa to the others and shook his head. "I'm sorry," he said. "I didn't mean to cause such a ruckus or harm your children." He sighed deeply and turned to Gus. "It's time I told you the truth. I was the agent you sent your music to."

Everyone gasped. Gus's legs began to shake and he slowly sat back down in his seat.

"When you sent me your song," Mr. Tom explained, "I thought it was terrific, and I gave it to the music producer I worked for. Then, one night while I was working late, I overheard him talking on the phone about a new song he'd just come across. I heard him say, 'Never mind where I got it, it's just the sound they need to get them back on top again.' He gave your song to another singing group to jump-start their stalled career."

Gus covered his face with his hands. Christina's mouth dropped open in disbelief.

"As I watched through the doorway," Mr. Tom continued, "he held up a sheet of paper while he was talking. I recognized it was your song since I had just received it in the mail a few days before. Then, I saw him open a small compartment in the top drawer and slip the song into it, hiding the evidence."

"Why didn't you stop him?" Will asked. "That was wrong!"

Mr. Tom looked at Gus. "I was afraid of the music producer, so I denied ever getting your song. He was a very powerful man in Detroit at that time. So, I snuck away and never told anyone," he added.

"I left the music business after that and became a night watchman," Mr. Tom said. "I eventually got a job at the Motown Museum. Then, I met you and heard your story. I felt terrible, but I never told you who I was. When the desk showed up as a donation, I recognized those lion-head drawer pulls. It was the desk that belonged to the music producer so many years ago."

"We discovered it was you in the basement the whole time," Christina said, "and you told Helene you didn't hear any noises."

Mr. Tom nodded. "I wondered if your song just might still be in that desk. I spent many nights in the basement moving things around to get to the desk. Once I did, I didn't know how to open the secret compartment. I tried to cover the noises I was making by saying I hadn't heard anything."

"But why didn't you just tell Gus the truth?" Grant asked.

Mr. Tom hung his head. "Because I was too ashamed," he said. "When I saw Grant come out of the room with the sheet music, I knew it was time for me to come forward and tell the truth, but I was scared, so I tried to get the sheet music from him."

Christina nodded to Grant. They walked over to Gus, who still looked stunned. Grant handed him the original sheet with the music on it.

"Here Mr. Gus," Grant said, "I believe this belongs to you."

Grant quickly recapped what had happened at the Motown Museum. "We didn't even know it was Mr. Tom who knew the truth about your song until we had all the clues."

"What clues?" Gus asked.

Grant reached into his backpack and showed Gus the taped-up photograph. "We've been getting pieces of photographs with notes on them for the last few days," he said. "They just kept appearing, and we kept trying to figure out who sent them and what they meant."

Grant set the photo on the table and turned it over to show Gus all the clues. Suddenly, Grant gasped. There in the lower right-hand corner of the picture was the logo of the Yankee Air Museum!

Grant's eyes met Christina's. They both turned to Mr. Joe. "It was you who sent the clues, wasn't it?" Grant asked.

Joe smiled, and tipped his Yankee Air Museum hat. "Yes, with the help of my very capable crew of course," he said, gesturing to the other men sitting at the table. The kids recognized Harry, Richard, and Wild Bill from the Yankee Air Museum.

"We've known Gus's story for a long time," Joe said. He shrugged. "When he told us about the noises in the basement and that Mr. Tom said he didn't hear anything, a red flag went up in my head. So, I looked up Mr. Tom on the Internet. He went by Tom Greasy back then. Through my research, I learned that he had been a talent agent at the same time Gus's song disappeared. When I found an article that the desk of a very powerful music producer who worked with Gus had been donated to the Motown Museum, I put two and two together and came up with the answer."

Joe patted Grant on the head. "So, when you kids seemed so interested in the noises in the basement, it seemed like the perfect time to put our little plan into action. I printed out Mr. Tom's picture, tore it up, and started sending you pieces to help you solve the mystery."

"That's quite a story," Papa said.

Gus gathered the kids in a group hug. "You don't know what this means to me," he said, choking back tears. "You've found my lost song after all these years!"

Helene looked at Mimi. "Are you thinking what I'm thinking?" she asked.

Mimi nodded and smiled.

"Of course, you'll perform it tonight at the Motown Review, won't you, Gus?" Helene asked.

Gus grinned. "I will, if these four kids will be my backup group!"

"Absolutely!" Christina cried, and the kids slapped high-fives.

24
IT'S SHOW TIME!

The air in Hart Plaza crackled with excitement in anticipation of the Motown Review and the chance to get a glimpse of some Motown greats who had sung and danced their way into music history.

Huge TV screens presented music videos of Smokey Robinson, Stevie Wonder, Diana Ross and The Supremes, Marvin Gaye, The Jackson Five, The Four Tops, and The Temptations.

The kids huddled backstage with Gus as he reviewed their dance steps. "Now, snap your fingers and sway your arms just so," he explained. "Now, step, touch, step, touch, scoop, scoop, step, turn."

Gus stepped back to watch Grant. "Put a little more spin into it, my man," he said. "That's it! And remember: flair, flash, and class!"

It was nearly show time. Gus peeked through a narrow opening in the curtain to view the waiting audience. He wiped the palms of his hands on his trousers, and looked over at the kids.

"I don't know if I can do this," he said, holding up his hands. "See? I'm so nervous my hands are sweating." He looked panicked. "This is just too much excitement for an old man."

Christina took his hand. "It's OK to be scared, Mr. Gus," she said. "Just pretend you're at the Motown Museum teaching the crowd the Temptation Walk." Then she had a thought. "Mimi always says to feel your fear and do it anyway," she added.

That made Gus smile. "Your grandmother is a very wise woman," he said.

Grant, Will, and Denielle cheered, "You can do it, Gus!"

The curtain rose. "And now," Helene said, "Let's give a warm welcome to our very own Gus and his backup group, The Detectives!"

The audience whistled and cheered. Once the music started, Gus felt right at home on the stage. The kids, grinning from ear to ear, sang "Doo wop, doo wop," and followed Gus's lead on the dance steps.

Newspaper and TV reporters took hundreds of photographs, lighting up the stage with bright flashes. They peppered Helene with questions. Mimi even overheard a famous music producer say that he was very interested in Gus, and would contact him to arrange a meeting.

Mimi leaned her head on Papa's shoulder. "I'm so proud of those kids," she said.

Just then, Grant decided to show off and add a little extra spin to his steps. "WHOOOAAAAA!" he shouted, as his feet became tangled. He struggled to regain his balance, swinging his arms wildly in the air.

Luckily, Will grabbed Grant just before he toppled over the edge of the stage! The crowd laughed and cheered.

"Well, I guess that's show biz!" Papa said, laughing.

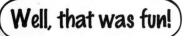

The End

Now...go to
www.carolemarshmysteries.com
and...

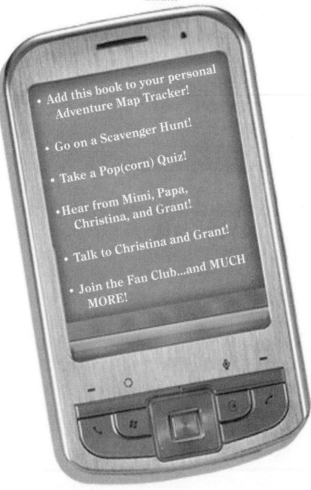

- Add this book to your personal Adventure Map Tracker!

- Go on a Scavenger Hunt!

- Take a Pop(corn) Quiz!

- Hear from Mimi, Papa, Christina, and Grant!

- Talk to Christina and Grant!

- Join the Fan Club...and MUCH MORE!

GLOSSARY

array: a large selection, or a group of things

baklava: a rich, sweet Greek pastry filled with chopped nuts and honey

chassis: base frame of a car or truck

docent: a lecturer or tour guide in a museum

enthralled: to be very impressed by someone or something

innovative: advanced or ahead of the times

multiplex: a building with multiple separate units

subconscious: a person's thoughts and feelings

truffles: creamy chocolate candy

SAT GLOSSARY

impugn: use words to attack something as being false or wrong

potent: strong, powerful

quibble: to argue over petty, unimportant things

raucous: unpleasantly loud and harsh

rebuff: to resist or refuse